USBORNE FIRST READING
Level One

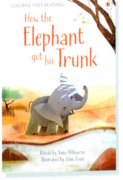

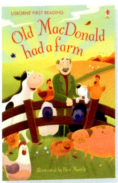

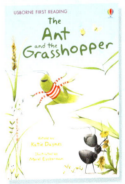

How the Rhino got his Skin

by Rudyard Kipling

Retold by Rosie Dickins

Illustrated by John Joven

Reading consultant: Alison Kelly

Once, the rhinoceros had skin as smooth as a pebble.

This story tells how
things changed.

3

Meet Rhino – a
rhinoceros with
a big horn

and BAD manners.

Rhino lived near
a man.

One day, the man
baked a cake.

sugar

currants

flour

Rhino stole it.

The man picked up
the crumbs.

9

It was a very hot day.

Rhino looked at the
cool sea.

Time for
a swim!

Rhino took off his skin and dived in.

SPLISH!

SPLOSH!

The man found the skin.

He filled it with crumbs.

Rhino put his
skin back on.

The crumbs itched
and tickled.

He rolled.

He rubbed.

Nothing
helped.

Then he got caught.

He lost his buttons.

21

Now Rhino has baggy
skin and a bad temper

and the man has
a smile.

Puzzles

Puzzle 1

Put the pictures in order.

A

B

C

D

E

Puzzle 2

Finish the rhyme.

...big bad snake!

...BIG mistake!

...big cornflake!

Puzzle 3

True or false?

 A  Rhino had good manners.

B  Rhino liked cake.

C  Rhino lost his buttons.

Puzzle 4

Spot five differences between the two pictures.

29

Answers to puzzles

Puzzle 1

Puzzle 2

Puzzle 3

<u>False</u>
Rhino had
<u>bad</u> manners.

<u>True</u>
Rhino liked
cake.

<u>True</u>
Rhino lost
his buttons.

Puzzle 4

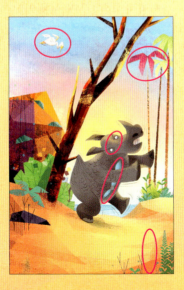

About the story

This story is from the book *Just So Stories* by Rudyard Kipling, which tells how animals came to be the way they are.

Designed by Sam Whibley
Series designer: Russell Punter
Series editor: Lesley Sims

First published in 2016 by Usborne Publishing Ltd., Usborne House, 83-85 Saffron Hill, London EC1N 8RT, England. www.usborne.com
Copyright © 2016 Usborne Publishing Ltd.

USBORNE FIRST READING
Level Two

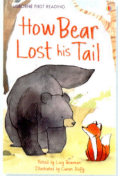

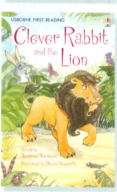

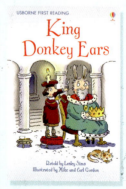